To ......................................................................

For being good.

MERRY CHRISTMAS!

From Santa

# Santa is coming to North Carolina

**Written by Steve Smallman**
**Illustrated by Robert Dunn and Jerry Pyke**
**Designed by Sarah Allen**

Published by Sourcebooks Jabberwocky, an imprint of Sourcebooks, Inc.
P.O. Box 4410, Naperville, Illinois 60567-4410
(630) 961-3900
Fax: (630) 961-2168
www.jabberwockykids.com

Library of Congress Cataloging-in-Publication data is on file with the publisher.

Source of Production: Worzalla, Stevens Point, WI, USA
Date of Production: September 2014
Run Number: 5002590
Printed and bound in the United States of America
WOZ 10 9 8 7 6 5 4 3 2

# Santa is coming to North Carolina

Written by Steve Smallman

Illustrated by Robert Dunn

sourcebooks
jabberwocky

# "Well?"

boomed Santa. "Have all the children of **North Carolina** been good this year?"

"Well...uh...mostly," answered the little old elf, as he bustled across the busy workshop to Santa's desk.

Santa peered down at the elf from behind the tall, teetering piles of letters that the children from North Carolina had sent him.

**"Mostly?"** asked Santa, looking over the top of his glasses.

"Yes...but they've all been **especially** good in the last few days!" said the elf.

DEC

| M | T | W | T | F | S | S |
|---|---|---|---|---|---|---|
|   |   |   |   | 1 | 2 | 3 | 4 |
| 5 | 6 | 7 | 8 | 9 | 10 | 11 |
| 12 | 13 | 14 | 15 | 16 | 17 | 18 |
| 19 | 20 | 21 | 22 | 23 | 24 | 25 |
| 26 | 27 | 28 | 29 | 30 | 31 |   |

"Jolly good!" chuckled Santa.
"Then we'd better get their presents loaded up!"

Even though the sack of presents was

# really, really big

and the elves were really, really small,

they seemed to have no trouble loading it onto Santa's sleigh.
Though how they managed to fit such a big sack into one little sleigh
even they didn't know. But somehow they did.

"Splendid!" boomed Santa. "We're ready to go!"

"Er...not quite, Santa," said the little old elf. "One of our reindeer is missing!"

# "Missing?

Which reindeer is missing?" asked Santa.

"The youngest one, Santa," said the elf. "It's his first flight tonight. I've called him and called him, but..."

Just then, a young reindeer strolled up, munching on a large carrot.

# "Where have you been?"

asked Santa.

But the youngest reindeer was crunching so loudly that it was no
wonder he hadn't heard the little old elf calling.

"Oh well, never mind," said Santa, giving the reindeer a little wink.
He took out his Santa-nav and tapped in the coordinates for North Carolina.
**"This will guide us to North Carolina in no time."**

Crunch!
Crunch!
Crunch!

With a flick of the reins and
a jerk of the harness, off they
went, racing through the sky.

"Ho, ho, ho!"

laughed Santa.

"We'll soon have these presents delivered to the Tar Heel State!"

Santa's sleigh flew through the starry night, heading south across the Arctic Ocean. On they flew, in the wintry air, crossing over Canada. In the wink of an eye, the sleigh was flying above the Great Lakes, over Ohio, and on to North Carolina. The youngest reindeer was very excited. He had never been away from the North Pole before.

They had just crossed over the Great Smoky Mountains
when, suddenly, they ran into a blizzard.
Snowflakes whirled around the sleigh.

# They couldn't see a thing!

The youngest reindeer was getting a bit worried,
but Santa didn't seem concerned.

## "In two miles..."

said the Santa-nav in a bossy lady's voice,

## "...keep left at the next star."

"But, ma'am," Santa blustered, "I can't see any stars in all this snow!"
Soon they were

# hopelessly lost!

Then, through the howling blizzard, the youngest reindeer heard a faint, ringing sound.

Ding-dong!

He looked over at the old reindeer with the red nose. But he had his head down.

(Red nose...I wonder who that could be?!)

Ding-dong!
Ding-dong!

Ding-dong!
Ding-dong!

# Ding-dong! Ding-dong!

There was that sound again, like church bells ringing. The youngest reindeer turned around to look at Santa. But Santa wasn't listening. He seemed to be arguing with a little box with buttons on it.

With a flick of the harness and a jerk of the reins, the youngest reindeer gave a sharp *tug* and headed off toward the sound of the bells, pulling Santa and his sleigh behind him!

"Whoa!"

cried Santa, pulling his hat straight. "What's going on?" Then, to his surprise, he heard the ringing sound.

"Well done, young reindeer!" he shouted cheerfully, "It must be the bells of the Morehead–Patterson Bell Tower at UNC-Chapel Hill. Don't worry, children, Santa is coming!"

Then, suddenly...

CRUNCH!

The sleigh hit something as it plummeted through the snow clouds. **"You have arrived!"** said the Santa-nav unhelpfully.

Finally, when the snow had died down and the clouds parted, Santa discovered exactly where they were...

...stuck, right at the very top of the **Christmas tree near the State Capitol building in Raleigh.**

"Everybody, PULL!"

The reindeer *pulled* with all their might until, at last, with a screeching noise, the sleigh scraped clear of the Christmas tree and Santa steered them safely past the City of Raleigh Museum, above Boylan Heights, over North Carolina State University, and down into Lake Johnson Park.

Luckily, there was
no real damage
done, but the packages
had all been jumbled
up. Santa quickly put the
presents back in order.

"All right," said Santa. "Thanks
to this young reindeer, I know
where we are now. Don't worry, children,

# Santa is coming!"

Santa drove his sleigh expertly from rooftop to rooftop all over North Carolina, popping in and out of chimneys as fast as he could go.

(Which was pretty fast for a chubby fellow!)

There were big chimneys in the Outer Banks, and small chimneys in Durham. He squeezed down thin chimneys in Charlotte, and plummeted down fat chimneys in Cary.

The youngest reindeer
was amazed at how quickly
they went. Santa never seemed to get
tired at all! And it looked like
the children of North Carolina were
going to be very lucky this year!
But the youngest reindeer was
starting to feel a bit weary,
and quite hungry too!

He piled them under the Christmas trees
and carefully filled up the stockings
with surprises.

In house after house, Santa delved
inside his sack for packages of
every shape and size.

Santa took a little bite out of each cookie, a tiny sip of milk, wiped his beard, and popped the carrots into his sack.

In house after house, the good children of North Carolina had left out a large plate of cookies, a small glass of milk, and a big, crunchy carrot.

From Greenville to Greensboro, from Asheville to Fayetteville, from Burlington to Wilmington, from Wake Forest to Winston-Salem, and ALL the places in between, Santa and his sleigh visited every house in North Carolina.

Santa delivered presents to Abigail, Addison, Aiden, Alexander, Andrew, Ava...the list went on and on! ...Violet, Wyatt, Xavier, Zachary, Zoe, Zybil.

(Zybil? Surely that must be a spelling mistake!)

Finally, Santa had delivered the last present on his long North Carolina list.

**"Great moons and stars!"** sighed Santa. "It's past midnight and my sack seems as heavy as ever! I hope I haven't forgotten anyone."

Santa opened his sack to check...but it was full of juicy, crunchy carrots!

Santa divided the carrots among all the reindeer.
"Good job!" he said, patting the youngest reindeer gently on the nose.

But the youngest reindeer didn't hear him...he was too busy munching!

Then it was time to set off for home. Santa reset his Santa-nav once more
to the North Pole, and soon they were speeding past Clingmans Dome, over Chimney
Rock, above Fort Bragg, and out over Cape Hatteras through the crisp, starry night.